Especially for Amy Jane, with love
~ M C B

To Basil Bahrani
~ T M

Original edition published in English by Little Tiger Press,
an imprint of Magi Publications, London, England, 2010.

LTP/1800/0230/0111 • Printed in China

Library of Congress Cataloging-in-Publication Data

Butler, M. Christina.
The smiley snowman / M. Christina Butler ; illustrations by Tina Macnaughton.
p. cm.
Summary: A bear, a fox, and a rabbit build a snowman, but
their efforts to keep it happy and warm almost bring its demise.
ISBN 978-1-56148-696-0 (hardcover : alk. paper)
[1. Snowmen--Fiction. 2. Bears--Fiction. 3. Foxes--Fiction.
4. Rabbits--Fiction.] I. Macnaughton, Tina, ill. II. Title.
PZ7.B97738Sm 2010
[E]--dc22
2010004916

The Smiley Snowman

M. Christina Butler   Tina Macnaughton

Good Books

Intercourse, PA 17534
800/762-7171
www.GoodBooks.com

The snowman was nearly finished. Little Bear and Small Fox lifted a big snowball on to his huge body.

"My turn!" cried Fluff Bunny. "Let me help!"

"Come on then, Fluff!" giggled Small Fox. "We can't leave you out!"

"Here we go!" cried Little Bear, lifting
him up, and Fluff gave the snowman
a great, big smile.

"Yippee!" squeaked Fluff. "He looks
really happy now! Hello, Snowman!"

"Let's go, Fluff!" shrieked Little Bear and
Small Fox, sliding down the hill.
   "But what about Snowman?" Fluff called.
"Don't worry, Snowman. I'll stay with
   you. What shall we play?"

So together they played
snowballs . . .

. . . and Fluff showed the
snowman how to do
headstands.

Then he told stories until
the sky grew dark and
snowflakes began to fall.

One by one, tiny lights started twinkling in the valley below.

"I have to go now," said Fluff. "Night-night, Snowman. See you tomorrow!"

Next morning the new snow sparkled bright.
"Wait for me!" gasped Fluff as he bounced
up the hill after Little Bear and Small Fox.
But the snowman looked sad and shivery.

"Oh no!" whispered Fluff. "What's wrong?"

"He looks cold to me," said Little Bear.
"He needs a hat!"

"I'll get a scarf!" cried Small Fox.

And off they went to see what they could find.

"This will warm him up!" giggled Little Bear
as they pulled the woolly hat and scarf
into place.

"What's happened to Fluff?" asked
Small Fox when they'd finished.
"I don't know," replied Little Bear.
"But there's something very strange
coming up the hill! Look!"

"What can it be?" asked Small Fox,
hiding behind Little Bear.
    A big, floppy thing with lumpy
bumps was shuffling nearer.
    Suddenly Little Bear laughed.
"It's Fluff!" he yelled. "He has a blanket!
Hold on, Fluff! We're coming!"

Together the friends pulled the blanket
up to the snowman. Then they tucked
it around . . . and pulled it up . . . and
wrapped it around again . . .

until only the snowman's big pebble
eyes were peeping out.

"He'll be nice and cozy now," said
Little Bear. "Come on, Fluff. Small Fox
has a new sled!"

Soon they were skimming
down the hill . . .

"We'll pull you, Fluff," laughed Little Bear. "Let's go and see Snowman."

with snowball fights on the way up—and down they went again—until Fluff was quite tired out and flopped back on the sled.

But something was wrong!

Drip! Drip! Drip! Drops of water were running down the snowman's face, and there were puddles of water everywhere!

"Our snowman's sinking!" Fluff yelled.

"He's melting!" cried Little Bear. "We'll have to make him cold again!"

They pulled off the blanket and threw Snowman's hat and scarf in the air. "Don't worry, Snowman," cried Fluff. "We'll save you!"

"More snow! More snow!" shouted Little Bear as they padded and packed, and smoothed and patted.

Soon the snowman was bigger
and better than before.
"Wow!" gasped Little Bear.
"We nearly lost him!"
"But why does he still look
so *sad?*" puzzled Fluff, staring
up at the snowman.

Fluff stretched his arms as far as he could
around the snowman's big snow body.
  "What's wrong, Snowman?" he asked
gently. "Please don't be so sad."
  "Look," whispered Small Fox.
"Something is happening . . ."

"He's smiling!" cried Little Bear suddenly.

"Fluff's done it!" shouted Small Fox.

"Snowman wasn't cold on the outside. He was cold on the inside!" Fluff grinned. "He just needed a hug!"

And as the stars twinkled in the clear night sky, they gave the snowman another hug, and his happy smile grew bigger than ever!